Merry Christmas!

♡ Shelley + Sarah 🐾

Merry Christmas Gregory, Jr!

"Aunt" Millie

Sarah Saves Christmas

Written By: Daniel Woll & Shelley Woll

Illustrated By: Shelley Woll

ISBN 978-1-937391-24-9

Published by Romeii Media Group

a division of Romeii LLC.

PO Box 146 Hudson, Wi

ebooks.romeii.com

Once upon a time there were two sisters.

Katie. She was eight.

Shelley. She was four.

They each had a Bernese Mountain Dog.

Katie's dog was eight, and very nice! They called her Sarah.
Shelley's dog was four and very nice, but naughty! They called him Bosko.
Christmas was the best time of the year for the little girls.
Three days before Christmas, Katie and Shelley were playing outside in the
snow with Sarah. Mom was inside taking a nap. Bosko decided to go inside.
Bosko liked to push things with his big paw. He pushed the door and locked
out the girls in the snowstorm.
"Whoo. Whooo. Whoooo," he said. "This is funny."

The little girls were cold. They began to yell.
"Bosko! Let us in! If we stay out here we will catch a cold and not be able to get out of bed and make a pie with Mom for Santa. And if Santa doesn't have his pie, he won't come. Do you want to ruin Christmas?!"
Sarah did not cry. She was so strong that she picked up a long, long branch with her mouth and tapped on Mom's upstairs window until she woke up.

The next day, Shelley and Katie were in the bathroom brushing their teeth.
Bosko followed them in.
They lived in a very old house.
Mom told them never to lock the bathroom door because it would stick.
Bosko reached with his big paw and pushed the lock button.

They were all locked in! The girls began to yell.
"We will be late for school and there will be a penalty. Christmas is ruined!"
Bosko said, "Whoo, whooo, whoooo."
That made the girls yell more.
Sarah was worried and starting barking as loud
as she could to get Mom's attention.
Mom heard Sarah's barks coming from upstairs
and ran to unlock the door for them.

On the day before Christmas, Mom helped the little
girls bake a Christmas pie for Santa.
While they were cooking the phone rang. "Oh no," Mom said. Grandma
needed a little help. Grandma was in the Veterans' Hospital.
"Katie, I must help Grandma. You are eight.
You must watch Shelley and the doggies. I will be back in one hour.
If you need help, call me on the cellphone."

She left.
Bosko and Shelley were bored.
They began to chase around the house.
Bosko knocked the Christmas pie off of the stove.
It went upside down on the floor. PLOP!

"OH NO!" screamed the girls. "Now Christmas is really ruined!"
"Call Mom!" said Shelley.
"No," said Katie. "I was supposed to be in charge. She will be angry!"
When the little girls cried, Bosko did too. "Whoo, whooo, whoooo," he said.
Sarah could not stand the crying. She pushed open the door and went next door
to Josephine's house. Joesphine was eighty-years-old and the nicest woman
in town. She had a kind heart, and lots of grandchildren who came to visit.
When she saw the tears in Sarah's eyes, she said, "What's the matter, Honey?"

Sarah raised one paw and pointed home. Josephine followed.
When she saw the mess, she cleaned it up. Then she went downtown
and bought a frozen pie, cooked it and set it out exactly where the
little girls' mom's pie had been.
When Mom returned, she was so busy that she never noticed.
That night the girls hugged Sarah. "Christmas is saved!" they said happily.

It was Christmas Eve, "What could go wrong now?" Katie thought.
The pretty tree was up, the pie was out and everything was ready.
Mom put the girls and their dogs to bed.
"Sleep tight," she said as she kissed the girls and patted the dogs.
Katie fell asleep. A noise woke her up. Shelley and Bosko were gone!
She heard laughing downstairs. Shelley and Bosko were
playing hide-and-go-seek around the Christmas tree!
"Stop!" she said.
Too late....

The tree fell over. "Christmas is ruined!" Katie screamed.
Shelley cried softly and Bosko whimpered,
"whoo, whooo, whooooo" Even Katie cried.
They tried to put the tree up but the girls were too
little and not strong enough.
Big Sarah came over and pushed. Sarah was five feet tall
when she stood on her hind legs. Up went the tree!

"Roof!" went Sarah. That meant, "GO. TO. BED"
The girls did. So did Bosko. Later that night, Santa came.
He ate some pie and then left lots of presents.

When the girls woke up, Shelley said, "This is the best Christmas ever!"
Katie said, "Sarah saved Christmas!"
Bosko said, "Whoo, Whooo, Whoooo!"
Sarah wagged her tail, crawled under the tree and took a nap.
She was smiling.

The End

About the Authors

Dan Woll is an author living in River Falls, Wisconsin with his wife Beth and their Bernese Mountain Dog, Bosko. He is the author of *North of Highway 8* and co-author of the political thriller, *Death on Cache Lake*. His writing is informed by his career as an educator and his mountaineering and cycling background as well as life in a household of four women-Beth, and daughters Jenny, Katie and Shelley.

Shelley Woll lives in Fort Collins Colorado where she graduated from Colorado State University. When she's not working, Shelley tries to get out and enjoy the outdoors as much as possible. Besides hiking and skiing with her dog Sarah, Shelley's passions include reading and writing.

Bosko is a beautiful Bernese Mountain Dog. He loves to play, run and snuggle with people. He comforted Grandpa Joe and Grandmas Ginny and Corinne when they were in care facilities. He would like to become a licensed therapy dog, but he is still too young and silly to pass the test. In the meantime, he pulls Dan in ski-joring races and patrols the neighborhood, checking on all of his dog friends.

Sarah the Bernese Mountain Dog
Hi, I'm Sarah! I was adopted from the Bernese Mountain Dog Club of the Rockies Rescue Group in 2008. When I'm not saving Christmas, my favorite things are swimming, being in the snow and playing with my best friend Dolly. I have gotten to travel lots of places since my mom adopted me, including Colorado, Alaska, California, and Wisconsin. When I was living in Alaska I even got to swim through an ice field one time! I hope you like my book and have a very merry Christmas. ***Woof!***